The spirit of Christmas
can happen to you
when you really believe
the way that kids do.

Like one child long ago
on a cold Christmas Eve
when all hope was lost,
he did believe.

His name was Siegfried,
and his faith shone bright
through the marvelous misfortunes
of one *Silent Night.*

'Twas Oberndorf, Austria,
in the year 1818.
The home of the Vaughn
family mice is the scene.

Siegfried, second youngest
of the family Vaughn mice,
sits cutting gold paper
in the same shape twice.

It's a bright Christmas star
for the top of the tree.
He does a good job
for his papa to see.

Papa Vaughn is a sailor
and he's long been away,
but his family's expecting
him home Christmas Day.

Lanky Lars, the eldest,
is directing the scene
while Tina helps Katrina
trim the fresh evergreen.

Roly-poly Popov
helps his mama bake treats.
He rolls out the dough
for the big cookie sheets.

And Mama holds the youngest,
her new baby Thor,
when they're summoned by the sound
of a rat-tat at the door.

The whole family hears,
and thrilled by the sound,
squealing "Papa! Papa!"
To the front door they bound.

But it isn't Papa hunched
before the family Vaughn mice;
it's Uriah, the landlord,
with a soul cold as ice.

The rat slithers in.
What a rogue of a gent!
"Season's greetings!" he says.
"Do you have the rent?"

"When Papa comes home ..."
begins Mama Vaughn.
The rat interrupts,
"Stop! Stop! Stop! Don't go on!

"You see, my dear lady,"
the sly rat begins.
He pretends to be sad,
but inside he grins.

"Such sad news I bear.
'Twas a storm we've to thank.
They found no survivors
when your husband's ship sank."

Mama lets out a cry
and Uriah presses near.
"I could help with your family
if you'd wed me, my dear.

I'm a man of some means,
stocks and properties to show.
You'd have no rent worries,
and I like kiddies so!"

He grabs Mama Vaughn,
throws his arms round her waist;
he gives her a kiss
much to her distaste.

This is the straw
that breaks the rat's back.
The family Vaughn mice
now spring to attack!

h, how the fur flies
s they tumble about!
here is kicking and biting
nd whiskers pulled out.

he big rat is stronger
nd about to win
hen Mama clouts his head
ith the rolling pin.

The rat spits and sputters,
and his eyes spin around.
Then out comes a howl,
a horrible sound!

"I'll have my revenge!"
he vows with a shout.
Then he forcibly kicks
the Vaughn Family mice out.

The night is now silent.
They are cold in the snow,
and the fatherless family
has no place to go.

Mama gathers her children.
'We've a storm here to weather.
Were Papa alive,
he'd say stick together."

Then Siegfried speaks up,
'Papa's not dead,

and when he comes home,
he'll bust that rat's head."

"Siegfried, look out!"
Mama Vaughn screams
as out springs a cat
from nowhere, it seems.

Panicked mice scatter
in every direction
seeking some place to hide,
some place for protection.

When the danger is passed,
they realize the cost.
There lie Siegfried's glasses,
but Siegfried is lost.

Bong! Bong! Bong!
the church bells toll.
A shrine near the church
holds the little lost soul.

Around him silent figures
seem frozen as can be.
Without the aid of glasses,
Siegfried cannot see,

this shrine holds a crèche
and the Christmas Child,
the *Holy Infant,*
so tender and mild.

Siegfried is freezing;
will he end this way?
He thinks of his father
and starts to pray.

"Oh, please, God,
I haven't been naughty.
Don't let me end up
a frozen mouse body."

It could have been chance
or carefully planned,
but it seemed at that moment
someone lent a hand.

For, out of the blue
and coming his way
are the family Vaughn mice
and a boy with a sleigh.

Siegfried hears them and squeals,
"That family is mine!"
And he gets so excited,
he falls out of the shrine.

His mama cries, "Siegfried!"
and so do the others.
There is hugging and kissing
from sisters and brothers.

Mama gives him his glasses
so Siegfried can see
the boy who befriended
his lost family.

The boy's name is Gustel.
He smiles with delight.
And in the boy's eyes
all is calm, all is bright.

"I live in this church
in a room that is nice.
You can all live with me
and be the church mice."

They go through the door
and, to their delight,
see people preparing
for Christmas this night.

Some deck the halls
with boughs of pine

while the choir sings praise
to that night divine.

But one thing, above all,
captures young Siegfried's eye
the gold pipes of the organ
reaching up to the sky.

And the voice of the organ,
as it sings with the choir,
lifts the little mouse
higher and higher.

Gustel stops at his door.
Siegfried looks back, and then
he says, "God's house is beautiful."
And the choir sings amen.

A star in the sky
shines a heavenly light
as Mama tucks her children
in bed for the night.

Their bellys are full.
Their cares seem to cease
while the family Vaughn mice
sleep in heavenly peace.

All except Siegfried
who tosses and turns.
An unsettled feeling
inside of him churns.

He climbs out of bed and says
"God, not to bother,
but I can't sleep.
I've been thinking 'bout Fathe

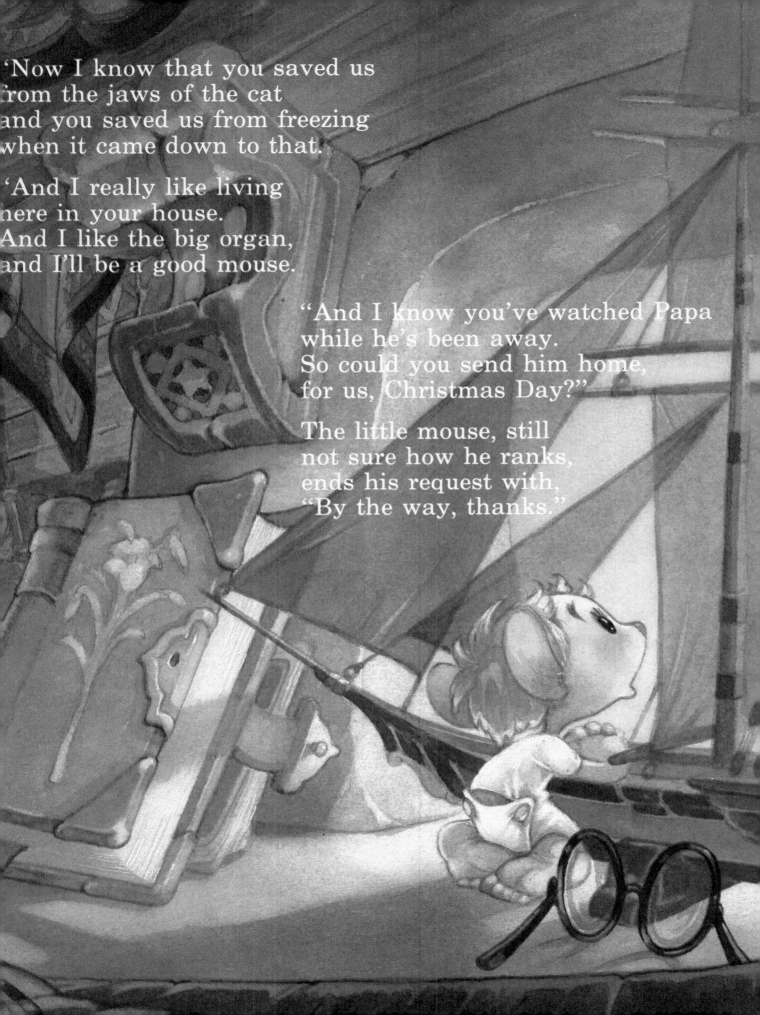

'Now I know that you saved us
from the jaws of the cat
and you saved us from freezing
when it came down to that.

'And I really like living
here in your house.
And I like the big organ,
and I'll be a good mouse.

"And I know you've watched Papa
while he's been away.
So could you send him home,
for us, Christmas Day?"

The little mouse, still
not sure how he ranks,
ends his request with,
"By the way, thanks."

Now who's that in the shadows,
in this room in God's house;
what sinister figure
is watching the mouse?

This ominous someone
in cloak and hat
is their villainous landlord,
Uriah, the rat.

He muffles a chuckle
inside of his shroud.
"Now, I will have
the *revenge* that I vowed.

"So you like the big organ.
Well, an organ needs bellows.
If it looked like mice chewed them,
you would be homeless fellows."

So, pleased with himself
he chuckles once more.
Then he slithers his way
through the bellows-room door.

There lie the bellows
made of leather and wood,
the things mice might chew
if they weren't being good.

The rat rips the bellows;
he chews and rips more.
But he stops when he sees
Siegfried standing in the door.

He cannot leave this witness
who's observed his attack.
So he snatches the child
and stuffs him in a sack.

He arrives at the docks
just before dawn
where he's going to drown Siegfried
when he meets Papa Vaughn.

Though his ship had sunk,
Papa Vaughn is all right.
He has been to his home
and found the mess from the fight.

So he corners the rat
and snarls, "What's going on?
Where's my wife and my babies?
Where's my family gone?"

Uriah denies knowing
but begins to perspire
when out pops Siegfried
screaming, "Uriah's a liar!"

Papa knows in a flash
what has come about.
So he draws back his fist,
and he knocks the rat out.

Christmas bells rang
as the family united.
All were happy;
Siegfried was delighted!

For not only had Papa
come home Christmas Day,
but the organist and priest
wrote a new song to play—

Not for the organ
but a song to sing,
of Joseph and Mary
and the newborn King.